Whose tail?

JEANNETTE ROWE

ABC Books

Whose tail?

crocodile's tail

Whose tail?

kangaroo's
tail

Whose tail?

fish's
tail

Whose tail?

pig's
tail

Whose tail?

tiger's tail

Whose tail?

horse's
tail

Whose tail?

MY
TAIL!

For Leyna and Ethan

  The ABC 'Wave' device and the 'ABC For Kids' device are
trademarks of the Australian Broadcasting Corporation and are
used under licence by HarperCollins*Publishers* Australia.

ABC
Books

First published in 2001 by ABC Books for the
AUSTRALIAN BROADCASTING CORPORATION
Reprinted by HarperCollins*Publishers* Australia Pty Limited
ABN 36 009 913 517
harpercollins.com.au

HarperCollins*Publishers*
Level 13, 201 Elizabeth Street, Sydney, NSW, 2000, Australia
31 View Road, Glenfield, Auckland 0627, New Zealand

National Library of Australia
Cataloguing-in-Publication entry
Rowe, Jeannette.
Whose tail?
ISBN 978 0 7333 0986 1.
1. Animals - Juvenile fiction I. Australian Broadcasting Corporation
II.Title.
A823.3

The illustrations were drawn with oil pastels on coloured paper.
Designed and typeset by Monkeyfish
Colour separations by PageSet, Victoria
Printed in China by RR Donnelley

5 4 3   13 14

This project has been assisted by the Commonwealth Government
through the Australia Council, its arts funding and advisory body.